HELPING YOUR BRAND-NEW READER

Here's how to make first-time reading easy and fun:

▶ Read the introduction at the beginning of each story aloud. Look through the pictures together so that your child can see what happens in the story before reading the words.

▶ Read the first page or so to your child, placing your finger under each word.

▶ Let your child touch the words and read the rest of the story. Give him or her time to figure out each new word.

▶ If your child gets stuck on a word, you might say, *"Try something, but the picture. What would* [...]

▶ If your child is still stuck, supply the right word. This will allow him or her to continue to read and enjoy the story. You might say, *"Could this word be 'ball'?"*

▶ Always praise your child. Praise what he or she reads correctly, and praise good tries too.

▶ Give your child lots of chances to read the story again and again. The more your child reads, the more confident he or she will become.

Text copyright © 2004 by Catherine Friend
Illustrations copyright © 2004 by Wong Herbert Yee

First edition 2004

Library of Congress Cataloging-in-Publication Data is available.

Library of Congress Catalog Card Number 2003069717

ISBN 0-7636-2331-8

2 4 6 8 10 9 7 5 3 1

Printed in China

This book was typeset in Letraset Arta.
The illustrations were done in
watercolor and ink.

Candlewick Press
2067 Massachusetts Avenue
Cambridge, Massachusetts 02140

visit us at www.candlewick.com

EDDIE THE RACCOON

CANDLEWICK PRESS
CAMBRIDGE, MASSACHUSETT

Catherine Friend ILLUSTRATED BY Wong Herbert Yee

Contents

NO EGGS FOR EDDIE

Introduction

This story is called *No Eggs for Eddie*. It's about how Eddie finds an egg and takes it and then finds more eggs. But then Big Chicken finds Eddie.

3

Eddie finds one egg.

4

Eddie takes the egg.

5

Eddie finds two eggs.

6

Eddie takes the eggs.

Eddie finds three eggs.

8

Eddie takes the eggs.

Big Chicken finds Eddie.

10

Eddie takes the eggs back.

EDDIE IN A JAM

Introduction

This story is called *Eddie in a Jam.* It's about how Eddie finds a jar of jam. He puts his paw and his tail in the jar. Yum, yum. But when he puts his nose in, Eddie gets stuck.

13

Eddie finds a jar of jam.

14

He puts his paw in.

Yum, yum, yum.

He puts his tail in.

Yum, yum, yum.

He puts his nose in.

Yum, yum, yum.

Oops!

EDDIE DIGS A HOLE

Introduction

This story is called *Eddie Digs a Hole*. It's about how Eddie digs with a spoon, a bucket, and a shovel. When the dirt lands on Big Chicken, Eddie runs!

23

Eddie digs with a spoon.

Dig, Eddie, dig.

Eddie digs with a bucket.

Dig, Eddie, dig.

Eddie digs with a shovel.

Dig, Eddie, dig.

Oh no!

Run, Eddie, run!

EDDIE AND LITTLE SKUNK

Introduction

This story is called *Eddie and Little Skunk*. It's about how Little Skunk chases Eddie, and how Eddie runs away until they go into a cave. Then they both run away.

Little Skunk chases Eddie.

Eddie runs away.

Little Skunk chases Eddie.

Eddie runs away.

Little Skunk chases Eddie.

Little Skunk chases Eddie into a cave.

Eddie and Little Skunk see a bear.

Eddie and Little Skunk *both* run away!